AUCTIONED OFF FOR MILKING

Fertile First Time Bimbo

Leandra Camilli

ISBN: 9798371015242
Imprint: Independently published

1st edition

CONTENTS

CHAPTER 1

I went up, reaching the top of the hill. Two men stood a couple of feet from me, watching me with the utmost attention. They were eyeing me, loving every curve and part of my body.

Why wouldn't they be acting like that? I was exposed. My skin wasn't protected by anything and I was naked from top to bottom.

The guy on the right, the one with hair falling to his shoulders, smiled without showing his teeth. It was more like a smirk, overflowing with his self-esteem. He had all the reasons to feel like that, of course.

His body was nothing short of stunning, making my pussy prickle with pleasure right now. I wanted him to fill me up with everything he had, but I didn't think something like that could ever happen.

I was being auctioned off because I was a bad fisherwoman, thinking that nobody would ever find out about my criminal activities. Now, I had a huge debt to pay and those two hunters knew everything about that.

They lived here on this island and made it theirs. It was their territory.

I was only a guest here.

My eyes couldn't stop roaming over his entire body, eyeing his muscles and scrutinizing them. The thing that I most wanted to do right now was to roam my hands over his shoulders, standing on my tiptoes because he was so much taller than me.

And I would also stand in front of the other guy. He was also much taller than me. If we were to hug each other, my arms would go under his and he would even be able to put his chin on top of my head. That was how significant the height difference between us was.

He wasn't smiling. I didn't know his name – something that I was going to have to rectify soon – but that didn't matter right now. What mattered was that he was turned on by what his eyes were seeing. There was no other way to put it. After all, his cock was already pressing up against his shorts. Should I even call it a pair of shorts? Sometimes, I found myself questioning that.

'Sometimes' because it felt like this auction was taking forever to finish. I didn't know if I was only imagining things, but sometimes, that was the thought that crossed my mind.

I wasn't drugged or anything of the sort. I was in the right state of mind. The only thing different was that I was naked and being auctioned off to the highest bidder. But even that was a lie.

Only three people were here on this tiny island: me and the two Australian men next to the bottom of the small hill that I was on right now.

The guy on the right waved his hand. "Alright, enough is enough with this. I think we should proceed to the best thing about this," he said before climbing up the hill and coming toward me.

My body was frozen up on the spot, with me finding it impossible to go anywhere. Even if it were possible, I wouldn't try to run away anywhere right now. After all, there weren't many options for me to run away to. Around the island, there was only the ocean. Nothing more than that.

It was isolated, to say the least.

"I agree," the guy on the right said before running after the first one, stopping by my side. After that, he positioned himself behind me, leaning down and breathing my scent.

Ripples of pleasure ran through my body. His hands on my shoulders were enough to put me into the right mood, and I could only imagine how big he was, my eyes darting down, my mind obsessed with the possibilities that would come with that.

"I know it feels like I always start this by doing this, but who can blame me for that? After all, you are one of the most beautiful women I've seen in my life. It's such a pity that you have to put yourself through this fake, useless auction. After all, I just want to get to the best part."

After that, he lowered his head a little more. Even though I couldn't look over my shoulder and see everything he was doing right now, I knew that he closed his eyes just to breathe in my scent.

He was obsessed with it.

My knees buckled, feeling weaker than they had ever been. My body inclined forward and I gasped, fearing that I was going to fall down the hill, but then he grabbed me, holding me up.

"Whoa there, Virginia. I'm not letting you fall down the hill like that. You are important to me even if, most of the time, you think you aren't."

His fingers dug deep into my skin. Turning me around, his eyes met with mine and I flicked my pupils to the right after finding his stare overwhelming. But if I was thinking that I was going to find refuge in the view of the ocean that surrounded us, I was only fooling myself.

After all, there stood the other Australian, and this was the one with longer hair. He looked like Thor from the Marvel movies, tall, and imposing, and his balls created a volume under his shorts.

It was enough to water my mouth and I wasn't exaggerating.

I couldn't stop looking down and he noticed that. Putting his finger under my chin, he lifted my head, making my eyes lock with his again.

"Every time I look at you, I think that you can only pay your debt after becoming our hucow. You are thinking the same thing, aren't you?" He asked, but there was no point in answering his question. After all, he already knew the answer.

I opened my mouth to say something. What was I going to say? I didn't know. The only thing that I was thinking about, or rather, obsessing over, was the size of his shaft, and I knew that it was already begging for me to take it into my mouth.

We could do that or proceed to the transformation. My body was going to be changed in ways I never thought possible.

CHAPTER 2

Mitchell had his own plans in mind for me right now, and he wasn't going to be held back by his buddy. Without saying anything, he pushed him to the side and away from me.

Planting his hands on my shoulders, he made me sit on the sand. It was hot thanks to the sunlight and a little uncomfortable, and I could feel my fingers treading through it.

He lowered his head, breathing in my scent.

"I just can't help myself. Every time I smell your scent, my mind goes crazy about you," he commented, smiling. And he then put his hand on my leg, running it on it. He pulled his hand up before finding my pussy, which was glistening with my orgasm.

I could feel it building up inside of me as well. When it showered me with it, everything would be as if it didn't exist.

He stopped when his finger was no more than some inches from touching my pussy. My pussy lips were already trembling with pleasure and I was so exposed I could only stay right where I was without being able to do anything. After all, I wasn't going to fight back against the pleasure that he wanted to reward me with.

Jonathan wasn't feeling too pleased with what happened. He sped up forward, fisting his hand and throwing his arm back. He was going to punch Mitchell, but then he smiled, showing us that he was only kidding.

He wasn't going to start a fight when we were almost reaching such an interesting point today. After all, the only thing that he was actually thinking about right now was how much he wanted to fill me up with his gargantuan shaft.

Mitchell returned his attention to me and didn't hold himself back this time before doing what he wanted. He began to rub my clit over and over, the movement slow.

He was dragging this out so that he could torment me. When I was on the verge of my moment of no return, he would stop. No denying it.

I had to close my eyes, arching my back. His finger was doing amazing things to my clit, and I was so close to coming. When I came, it would be one of the most shattering experiences of my existence, and I wasn't exaggerating.

He was breathing on top of me. I could feel the hot air coming out of his nose. And there was also something else my attention was being divided with. The sound of skin rubbing on skin. It was coming from my left side, and I knew that could only be Jonathan.

I didn't have to open my eyes to know he was jacking off.

Moaning and groaning, I was also huffing and by the time this was over, I didn't know if I would still be the same person.

Mitchel sped up his finger, getting me to that moment of no return. And, it happened. My body began to shake and I felt that wave of pleasure coursing through my body. It reached every cell in it, and I knew that this was over – at least, for the time being.

There were still so many more things to happen now, of course. I reopened my eyes, finding Mitchel still straddling me. His dick was bigger now than before, something that I hadn't thought possible. I thought that he was already at full mast before.

He flicked his eyes down. "That's the only thing you want right now, isn't it?" He asked, murmuring.

But I didn't have time to answer his question. After all, Jonathan was already stepping forward, his hand still shooting up and down, fapping. He wanted to cover me with his come, and I couldn't wait until he did that.

Jonathan positioned himself so that he was in the perfect place to do that. My eyes could only focus on the gland of his cock, imperious, the slit opening.

"Fuck," he groaned, the slit opening a tiny bit more before his milk began to spurt out. One rope after the other, he started to cover my body with his release, and, for me, it was as good as what I had before.

So good I knew my orgasm was already growing again. It wouldn't take too much to bring me to that point of no return again, making me climax once more.

That was the reason why I didn't stop myself before shooting my hand to my clit, rubbing it on it for a brief moment. After that moment, I scratched my clit until it happened, my body shaking.

When it was over, I reopened my eyes and found Jonathan and Mitchell still gazing at me. They were still smiling confidently.

"Damn, Virginia," Jonathan said before beginning to walk around me. Still circling me, he said, "we knew that you were hungry for this, but we didn't think that you were such a slut. Maybe that's something we should do something about, or maybe we should just enjoy this for as long as we can."

"Of course, that would still leave your debt. You have to do something about that. You have to pay us. Do you agree to become our property so that we can do whatever we want to you?"

I didn't even have to think about it much. I just nodded, lurching forward and throwing my arms around his legs, burying my head between his feet.

"I'm going to do everything I want for you two, my dear Masters."

"Dear?" He asked, chuckling. "I think that there is something about us you don't understand."

CHAPTER 3

And, there was. I wasn't only going to become their property, but also something else. I was going to become theirs for the rest of my life, and my mind was already thinking about how good that was going to be.

He grabbed my hand and took me down the hill. The island was small, and we could see some trees, some shrubs, more sand, and that sort of thing. It was homey, but I wouldn't spend much time here. If it weren't for the mistake that I made before, I wouldn't be in this place. That was the truth.

We went to a cave. It was a big, sprawling cave. Just looking inside it, I couldn't see what was beyond us, and I still wasn't afraid. No matter what happened here, I knew that Mitchell and Jonathan were going to keep me safe. *For their own pleasure,* of course, but they were still going to keep me safe here.

They both chuckled, taking me deeper inside the cave. Where are we going? I asked myself, and I realized that I wasn't going to get the answer to that question no matter how much I tried.

A few seconds after that, we stopped. They threw me forward and I fell on my ass on the ground. It was made of hard rock and it hurt like hell, but it didn't bother me and it also didn't make me furious at them. If anything, it made me feel exactly what I wanted to feel right now.

Like their property and nothing else.

I looked up and noticed that Mitchell was holding something in his hand. I didn't even realize that he had enough time to take it with him. I didn't even think that he was going to use it on me, but he showed me that there were so many things about him I didn't know.

A butt plug. It was made of metal. Some kind of metal. I didn't even know what kind of metal it was, and it didn't matter. It was round at the base and it became sharp at the other end. There was also a smaller part where Mitchell could put his fingers around it so that he could put it inside of me or take it out anytime he wanted to.

Despite how dark the cave was, the butt plug was still glistening as if there was some kind of liquid covering it. It was kind of odd, but I didn't think much about that. What I was thinking about was that they were going to fuck my asshole just like they were going to fuck my pussy as well.

I was kind of disappointed that the butt plug didn't have anything else going for it. It didn't have a tail or anything of the sort. It was just the butt plug, but it was going to do the work that it was supposed to. It was going to stretch me wide and was going to prepare my asshole for their entry.

He smiled, moving his finger as he asked me to turn around and lift my ass. There was nothing I could do to change his mind about that, so I obeyed. I lifted my ass up and he padded to me. He positioned himself behind me and then began to press the butt plug into my anus. I could feel it coming inside of me and stretching my walls in ways I didn't think possible.

I had to close my lips as tightly as possible and grit my teeth. There was just so much pain coming from my asshole right now, and I didn't think that it was going to subside as long as he was still easing the butt plug inside my asshole.

After a while, he moved his hand away and I knew that he was done with that. He didn't feel that there was any more need to put the butt plug deeper into my rectum.

After he took some steps away from me, I realized that the pain I was feeling before was not going away. It was still around the same intensity as before, and it also gave me more pleasure than I thought I was going to feel.

Jonathan cackled, pointing his finger at me as if we were in school and he was my bully. "Look at her! Virginia looks so stupid with the butt plug in her asshole. It doesn't matter how much we humiliate her and show her that she is nothing to us. She actually enjoys that."

He was mocking me, but that was okay. Right now, I was thinking and wondering when they were finally going to make me go through the transformation. After all, they had said before that my debt would only be paid when they could milk me. They had mentioned something about me becoming a hucow, a person who could produce milk and more of it until nothing was left of my body.

My mouth was already watering again just thinking about that.

Then, Jonathan lowered his shorts. What he said before did make me feel humiliated, but I didn't say anything about it. Not to mention that, with his dick springing free like that, I could only focus on that, my tongue running from one end of my mouth to the other.

He closed his fingers around that massive manhood, showing it to me.

"You want this so much right now, don't you?" He asked and I crawled over to him. Of course, that was what I wanted so much right now, to the point of making my heart race, and I wasn't going to hide that.

He put his hand in front of me, palm open, stopping me. Whatever he thought that I should do right now, he obviously wanted me to take my time.

"You are allowed to give it a little lick, but nothing more than that. It's going to be an appetizer," he announced, some pre-come seeping out of the slit. "Do you see my pre-come? It's what's going to change you into a hucow. After you taste it, your body will begin to change rapidly, and then you will finally become only ours."

CHAPTER 4

And I just couldn't stop pretending I would do anything to make that happen. So, without giving it another thought and as soon after he moved his hand away, I put my tongue out and licked the drop of his pre-come that was next to his slit.

He let out a little moan of pleasure and I basked in the taste of his pre-come. It was delicious and I could lick so much more of it if only he would allow me to do so. But the moment he realized I was lurching forward again to do that, he put his hand in front of me, palm open.

Smirking, he said, "what do you think you're doing? Your transformation is already happening and we want to keep our distance from you as it finishes."

I didn't think that it was going to start so soon, but Jonathan was right about everything. As soon as he mentioned that, my body began to change, grow, bigger with every passing second, and I knew that it wasn't much longer now until I was a hucow.

The good thing was that I wasn't wearing any clothes right now. Otherwise, they would be ripping to shreds right before my eyes. If they were expensive, I would feel so bad that I spent so much money on them.

But it wasn't like I would even have much money for that, anyway.

Nipples growing bigger by the second. They were already looking so swollen, one of the reasons why Jonathan and Mitchell let out a breath of pleasure, focusing only on me.

Milk was already being produced in my body. They licked their lips, thinking how much they were going to enjoy it as soon as they could have their lips all over it.

After that, my ass ballooned to a level I didn't think possible, and it was rounder and more pliable. Those Australian hunters were going to have a field day with it, I thought without hiding the smile that spread on my face.

My thighs grew in size too, thicker, heavier, just like it was happening with the rest of my body. I didn't know if this was going to be what was going to happen, but I felt that it was going to be impossible for me to walk around like I normally did after the transformation was over.

Even more milk was being produced inside of me. After all, I could feel my boobs aching already. The good thing was that I was already kneeling on the ground and wasn't standing. Otherwise, I would fall over on my boobs. They were so heavy and the nipples were so much longer now that, even though I was doing everything in my power to keep them from touching the ground, it was still happening.

A few seconds after that, when I was already panting, the transformation was over and Jonathan and Mitchell could only bask in what their eyes were witnessing.

So, this was what my body looked like after the transformation was over, and they loved that. They enjoyed seeing me in the humiliating position I was now at, their shafts growing bigger.

Following that, Jonathan was the first one to approach me. His steps were slow as he came to me. He then got on his knees and put his hands on my shoulders. He put his weight into his arms and made me lie down on the ground. The hard rocks hurt me, but it was okay. I couldn't be bothered much by that, experiencing this hunky Australian straddling me.

His eyes went up and down, enjoying what he was seeing.

He took in a deep breath, his finger running around my boob. I could feel it moving around my pliable breast, and I could only wonder what he could do with it that could make me come without doing anything out of the ordinary.

He turned his head to look at his buddy and Mitchell nodded. They didn't say anything, but I could more or less understand what their stare was about. Jonathan had asked him if it was okay for him to be the first one to milk me.

And as a side note, this was all bringing me so much pleasure that, for a moment, I forgot about the butt plug still inside my anus. After all, when they were finished milking me and fucking my pussy, they were going to take the virginity of my anus too, and my mind was already obsessing over that happening.

Jonathan moved down, lowering his head a few seconds after that. He closed his fingers around my boob and put my nipple into his mouth. For a moment, he didn't do anything, just running his tongue around my nipple, enjoying this a lot more than he should be.

"Please, milk me, Master," I let out a moment after that and he curved up the corner of his lips.

"Milk you? There are many more things I'm going to do to you," he said before beginning to rub his dong on my pussy, showing me that he was already thinking about fucking me there, too. To be honest, my mind was already wondering how that was going to happen."

He pressed his fingers on my nipple, drawing out the milk. And if I thought that Mitchell was going to stay still and watch this as it happened, I was only fooling myself. He began to jerk off while his eyes witnessed what his buddy was doing, and I could tell that he was enjoying that as if he was doing it himself.

In the meantime, I couldn't help myself, shooting my hand down and finding my clit. After that, I began to rub it over and over, and I knew that I was going to keep doing that until I climaxed.

And it was going to happen so much more quickly than before because Jonathan was milking me until I was dry.

CHAPTER 5

Jonathan was still milking me minutes after that, and part of me thought it wasn't going to end. I could see it in his eyes, how much he was enjoying this. He was enjoying this so much that he pressed his fingers into my boob the moment he realized that it was already drying up. He had to have those last drops that were still in my udders.

He pulled his head back, his eyes flicking to the right. There was still my other boob for him to play with, and I knew that he was only thinking about that.

He didn't waste any time, moving until he was easing my other nipple into his hungry mouth. His lips closed around it and he began to draw out all the milk. In the meantime, Mitchell was still jerking off, and I knew that he wasn't far from reaching his climax. When he did, he would shoot his milk all over me, and my body and mind were already thinking about how that was going to happen.

Jonathan, in the meantime, was moving on to do something else. After all, he was extracting all the milk that was in my breast, and he still had to plunge deep inside of me with his gargantuan shaft.

He pulled his head back up, watching me for a few moments before putting my legs over his shoulders. After that, he lined up his prick to my cunt, and I knew that he was going to penetrate me right now.

He took in a deep breath, easing his dick inside of me. He

was the Alpha male between the two of them, I could tell that from the way that he was doing this without asking for Mitchell's permission. He didn't need it.

He plunged deep inside of me without even announcing he was going to do that, and I could feel him already touching the end of my tunnel. He was all the way in there, and I could only wonder when he was going to start to ram in and out of me.

Without even showing me any signs he was going to do that, he began to roll his hips, and I could only groan and moan. Doing that and after I was rubbing my clit over and over before, I knew that it wasn't much longer until I was climaxing.

And, that happened only a few seconds after that, and the best thing about it was that it was happening at the same moment as Jonathan was unloading his come inside of me.

I was fertile and we were doing this without him using his condom, so we knew he was knocking me up. Huffing, he stayed inside of me to make sure that not even a single drop of come was going to come out, and I was happy he was doing that, so much so that I couldn't stop smiling.

A few seconds after that, Jonathan finally pulled out, and I realized that there was still Mitchell's turn. His eyes told me that he was thinking about fucking my asshole instead of my pussy, and I was joyful about that.

After all, the butt plug was still inside my anus and they had to do something about it, too. And they were going to. Mitchell made me go on all fours in the cave and looped his fingers around the handle before pulling the butt plug out of my dark tunnel.

He did that without making a fuss about it and it came out with a plop that reverberated in the cave. He examined the butt plug in his hand for a little while before tossing it over his shoulder.

Planting his hands on my ass, he studied my anus for some time before pulling me toward him. He didn't even look at Jonathan, who was still far from looking spent. After all, right now he was thinking about how he was going to enjoy when he was fucking my anus, too.

Or maybe he was thinking that that part of me belonged only to Mitchell. Whatever the case, I knew that he was still obsessing over the idea of destroying every part of me.

Mitchell wasted no time before easing himself inside of me, the movement slow. He was taking his time and I enjoyed that he was doing that. I wished that there was something for me to grab and hold onto, but there wasn't. My fingers could only scratch and feel the hard rocks under me.

When he was also inside of me, I had to grit my teeth. So much pain and it was overwhelming. He began to pound in and out of me without showing any mercy, and when he found his desired pace, he was destroying my insides, his balls slapping against my ass.

Perhaps the most interesting thing about that was that he could only come inside of me, and my mind was already obsessing about how that was going to happen. He was going to fill my asshole with his milk, and it was going to be one of the most amazing experiences I ever had in my life.

A few seconds after that, he stopped, his dick erupting inside of me, and I could only moo and groan, my eyes closing. I knew that this was going to take me over the edge and that I was going to climax, but I still didn't think that it was going to shatter all my expectations.

He stayed inside of me even after that and even though I was still doing everything in my power not to collapse on the ground, that was still what happened and it was the only reason why he wasn't inside of me anymore.

After that, he gave my ass a slap, telling me that I was still his and this wasn't over yet.

EPILOGUE

I felt that all of that happened eons ago even though it couldn't be a bit more than some months. After all, I was pregnant and my belly was huge, but I was still a little far from giving birth.

One amazing thing about this was that the transformation and being milked paid off my debt and I didn't have to worry about that anymore.

I was still naked and those Australian men could do whatever they wanted to me. One more thing about me being pregnant was that I had much more libido than before, one of the reasons why Jonathan wasted no time before popping up behind me.

He knew what I wanted, so he didn't stop himself before doing it. Since I was pregnant, he had to be more careful than he would be in other circumstances, but it was okay and he was already inside of me a few moments after that.

The difference was that this time, he was inside my asshole, filling me up with it, and it was one of the most rewarding experiences of my life. Was he bigger than Mitchell? I didn't know. They were about the same size, but one might be thicker than the other.

Now that he was inside of me, he lowered his head, his lips murmuring into my ear, "you are pregnant and craving more sex. That's what you want, isn't it?"

I nodded. It was the only thing I could do right now. That and pushing myself slightly back so that I was pressing harder against him, and his junk was pressing against my ass, too.

I wanted to feel as much of him as possible right now and knew that he was thinking the same thing.

"Gosh, even after all this time and fucking you so much, you are still unbelievably tight," he murmured, rolling his hips, and his pace was frenetic from the get-go. I could only try to match him thrust for thrust, and I knew it wasn't going to be enough. After all, he was so relentless, and even though he could come at any time, he was going to drag this out so he did it when Mitchell was watching. The latter was fishing not too far from us, but we knew that the noises we were making were going to announce what we were doing to him.

It happened just like we predicted, and when his eyes noticed what we were doing, he came rushing right over. Instead of showing jealousy, he put his fingers around his shaft and began to jack off, the movement of his hand lazy.

"Jesus, guys I know that you were going to have fun this morning, but didn't think that it was going to happen so quickly. I thought that I was going to have a little bit of time while fishing."

That was what he said, but we knew that he wasn't complaining about anything. After all, he was still jacking off and enjoying what his eyes were witnessing.

After that, Jonathan came inside of me and it was like bliss. I couldn't help but wonder if only one heir was going to be enough or if they were going to request more in the coming years.

I couldn't see myself living anywhere else, after all.

End of Book 1

My top series starters:

1. Hucow Flavor
2. Cowboys' Lucky Age Gap
3. Condemned to the Hucow Prison
4. Leaky Bimbo

5. Peculiar Dairy

Thank you for reading this story. Leave your review. Your feedback helps me immensely!

SIMILAR BOOKS

SERIES - Hucow for White Collars

1. Milked by Lawyers

2. Milked by Doctors

3. Milked by Engineers

4. Milked by Directors

5. Milked by Managers

SERIES - Fertile Only

1. Bumping the Teacher

2. Bumping the Midwife

3. Bumping the Farmhand

4. Bumping the Sinner

SERIES - Mafia Cowboys

1. Fertile for the Cocky Italians

2. Tied Up for the Cocky Italians

3. Serving the Cocky Italians

SERIES - Historical Hucows

1. Milked by Cavemen

2. Milked by Dukes

3. Milked by WW2 Soldiers

4. Milked by Kings

5. Milked by Princes

SERIES - Hucow for Blue Collars

1. Milked by Plumbers

2. Milked by Firefighters

3. Milked by Policemen

4. Milked by Electricians

5. Milked by Miners

SERIES - Welcome to my Harem

Joining his harem means obeying all of his rules. How much do they want his *big surprise*?

1. Bimbo Magic

2. When he Creams

3. Christmas Comes

4. Christmas Cream

5. Holiday Milking

6. Don't Pull Out

ABOUT THE AUTHOR

Leandra Camilli's obsession? Writing dirty, steamy stories that make her readers drool. She loves her Alpha males, hucows, sissies, and futas. If you're looking for those kinds of books, look no further.

With a cup of coffee on her table and warm socks on, she writes almost every day. Leandra Camilli has featured in several top 100 categories in the store, and she publishes weekly.